Zara
the Starlight
Fairy

Special thanks to Narinder Dhami

ISBN 978-0-545-27046-5

12 11 10 9 8 7 6 5 4 3 2 1   11 12 13 14 15/0

Printed in the U.S.A.   40

This edition first printing, July 2011

Zara
the Starlight
Fairy

by Daisy Meadows

SCHOLASTIC INC.

New York   Toronto   London   Auckland
Sydney   Mexico City   New Delhi   Hong Kong

The Night Fairies' special magic powers
Bring harmony to the nighttime hours.
But now their magic belongs to me,
And I'll cause chaos, you shall see!

In sunset, moonlight, and starlight, too,
There'll be no more sweet dreams for you.
From evening dusk to morning light,
I am the master of the night!

Contents

A Star is Born!

"This telescope is huge, Kirsty!" Rachel Walker said to her best friend, Kirsty Tate. "I can't wait to look at the night sky."

"It's going to be amazing," Kirsty agreed as they stared up at the enormous silver telescope.

The girls were spending a week of summer vacation with their parents at Camp Stargaze, which had its very own observatory for studying the stars. The observatory was a square, white building with a large dome on top, and charts and pictures of the night sky hanging on the walls. In the middle of the observatory stood the gigantic telescope. Professor Hetty, the camp astronomer, was explaining to Rachel, Kirsty, and the other kids about the stars and constellations.

"As you know, this area was chosen for Camp Stargaze because we can get really clear views of the night sky from here," Professor Hetty reminded them. She was a happy, round-faced woman with twinkling blue eyes and a mop of red hair. "Have any of you ever done a connect-the-dots picture?"

Everyone nodded.

"Well, a constellation is a lot like connect-the-dots!" Professor Hetty explained with a smile. "A constellation is made of individual stars that you join together to make a picture, just like with connect-the-dots. Even though the stars look close together to us here on Earth, sometimes  they're really millions of miles apart! Let's take a look, okay?"

Professor Hetty pressed a button on the wall. There was a noise overhead, and Rachel and Kirsty glanced up to see a large section of the domed roof slide back smoothly. This revealed the dark, velvety night sky. Sparkling silver stars twinkled here and there like diamonds in a jewelry box. Everyone gasped and clapped.

"Wonderful!" Professor Hetty said eagerly. "I never get tired of looking at the night sky. It's so magical."

Rachel nudged Kirsty. "Professor Hetty doesn't know just how magical the nighttime really is!" she whispered.

Kirsty smiled. When she and Rachel had arrived at Camp Stargaze, Ava the

Sunset Fairy had rushed from Fairyland to ask for their help. The girls had learned that Ava and the six other Night Fairies made sure the hours between dusk and dawn were peaceful and happy. Their job was easier with the help of their satin bags of magic fairy dust.

But while the Night Fairies were enjoying a party under the stars with their fairy friends, Jack Frost had broken into the Fairyland Palace with his goblins. The goblins had stolen the magic bags that were hidden under the Night Fairies' pillows. Then, with a wave of his ice wand, Jack Frost had sent the goblins and the bags spinning away from Fairyland—all the way to the human world. Jack Frost's plan was to cause nighttime trouble for both fairies and humans, but Rachel, Kirsty, and the Night Fairies were determined not to let that happen.

"I wonder if we'll meet another Night Fairy today," Kirsty murmured to Rachel as they all lined up to look through the telescope. "I'm so glad we found Ava's and Lexi's magic bags, but we still have five more to go!"

"Remember, we have to let the magic come to us," Rachel reminded her.

The girls' new friend Alex was first to use the telescope, and Professor Hetty showed her how to look through the eyepiece. Alex peered into the telescope eagerly.

"Everything looks so close!" She gasped.

"Can you see any pictures in the stars, Alex?" asked Professor Hetty.

"I think I see something. . . ." Alex leaned in closer to the telescope. "Oh!" She burst out laughing. "I can see a constellation shaped like a toothbrush!"

"Good job," said Professor Hetty. "And those of you who aren't using the telescope should also be able to see it, if you look hard enough." Rachel and Kirsty gazed intently up at the sky.

"Oh, there it is!" Kirsty exclaimed, pointing out the toothbrush of stars to Rachel. "And it even has bristles!"

"Lucas, it's your turn," Professor Hetty said.

Lucas, another one of Rachel and Kirsty's friends, took Alex's place at the telescope. He studied the sky for a few minutes and then turned to Professor Hetty.

"That constellation near the toothbrush looks like a pair of pajamas," he said with a grin.

"Right again!" Professor Hetty smiled. "Did you see the slipper constellation, too, just below the pajamas, Lucas?" Lucas looked again.

"Yes, I can see it now," he said. "It really is like connect-the-dots!"

After Lucas had finished, it was Rachel's turn.

"I'll change the angle of the telescope a little, Rachel," Professor Hetty told her. "Then you should be able to see something different."

Rachel looked through the glass eyepiece. At first, she was surprised. The stars looked so close and were so bright! Then, as her eyesight adjusted, she saw the constellation shaped like a slipper that Professor Hetty had mentioned earlier.

"This is amazing!" Rachel gasped.

"Can you seé any other constellations, Rachel?" Professor Hetty asked.

Rachel stared at the night sky. For a moment she couldn't see anything new, and then all of a sudden she noticed that some of the stars seemed to be grouped together in the outline of a face. The face had spiky hair, a spiky beard, and even a pointy nose.

"I think I see a face," Rachel said hesitantly.

"A face?" Professor Hetty sounded very surprised. "I wasn't expecting that!" She gazed up at the night sky, trying to spot it for herself. Meanwhile, Rachel frowned. That face in the stars looked familiar. . . .

"Aha, I see it now!" Professor Hetty exclaimed. "And look, everyone — a star has drifted away from the toothbrush constellation to be part of the face. We're actually seeing a new constellation forming in front of our very eyes. How amazing! I've never seen anything like it!"

"Kirsty, look at this!" Rachel said

quickly, moving aside to let her friend take her place at the telescope.

Kirsty took a good look at the constellation. The drifting star settled into its new place and became part of the face's spiky beard. Kirsty's eyes widened as she realized exactly who it was.

The face constellation was Jack Frost!

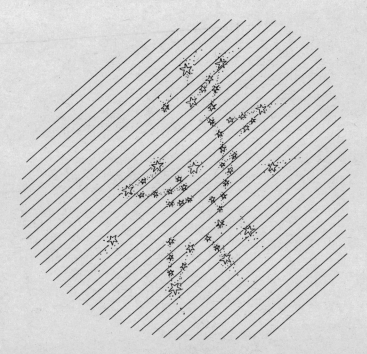

Zara Zooms In

"Jack Frost's face couldn't be a
real constellation, could it?" Kirsty
murmured to Rachel as they followed
Professor Hetty and the others out of the
observatory.

"Well, Professor Hetty seems to think
it is," Rachel replied. The professor was
so excited by the new constellation that
she hadn't stopped talking about it. "But
we know that Jack Frost must be using

the Night Fairies' magic to create chaos in the night sky."

Outside the observatory, Peter, one of the camp counselors, was waiting to introduce the evening activity. Immediately, Professor Hetty began telling him about the new constellation.

"And look, Peter, some stars are moving from the other constellations to join it!" she explained.

Rachel and Kirsty glanced upward. Several more stars had detached themselves from the pajamas constellation that Lucas had spotted earlier. Now they were floating across the sky! As the girls watched, the stars positioned themselves on Jack Frost's face, forming his familiar, icy grin.

"Okay, everyone, we're going to have

an orienteering race this evening," Peter told them. "In orienteering, you use the starts above as your guide, just like real explorers."

There was a murmur of excitement.

"Oh, great," said Kirsty. "We did orienteering when we visited that adventure camp, didn't we, Rachel?"

Rachel nodded. "It's fun," she agreed. "And it'll give us a chance to look around and try to find out what Jack Frost is up to!" she added in a low voice.

"First, get into pairs, and I'll give you a map of the constellations and a compass," Peter explained. "You should use them to find three locations within the camp. Each location name is the clue to a puzzle. Then, when you get to the last location, there will be a surprise waiting!"

"But you'll have to be quick," Professor Hetty called as she and Peter began handing out the compasses and maps. "This is a great night to be out under the stars because we can watch this new constellation forming. But if you take too long, more stars will have moved, and you may not be able to find your way!"

Kirsty looked up at the night sky again. The outline of Jack Frost now had a neck and the beginning of shoulders.

"At this rate, there won't be any constellations left in the sky except Jack Frost!" she told Rachel.

Rachel looked upset. "That would be awful!" she exclaimed, as her eye was caught by another sparkling star floating across the dark sky.

But this time the star didn't join the Jack Frost constellation. Instead, it suddenly plunged down toward the earth, leaving a trail of silver sparks behind it like a firework. Rachel clutched Kirsty's arm.

"Kirsty, I think that might be a shooting star!" she gasped.

As the two girls watched, the star spiraled downward and disappeared behind the observatory. No one else had noticed because they were too busy studying their maps.

Kirsty and Rachel slipped away quietly and ran to the observatory, their hearts thumping with excitement.

"Girls," called a clear, tinkling voice, "I'm over here!" And suddenly a tiny fairy popped out from behind the observatory.

"It's Zara the Starlight Fairy!" Rachel said.

"Hello, Zara," said Kirsty. "Welcome to Camp Stargaze!"

Zara smiled as the girls rushed over to her. She wore an oversize T-shirt scattered with stars, black leggings, and silver shoes. She also had on a silver

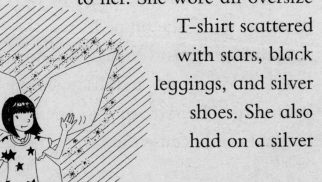

star bracelet and matching necklace.

"Yes, it's me," she replied. "And I'm sure you've noticed that Jack Frost is using my magic star dust to move all the stars around?"

Kirsty and Rachel nodded.

"Jack Frost is so vain, he wants a big picture of himself in the sky every single night!" Zara explained. "So he's stealing stars and ruining all the beautiful constellations. That means ships won't be able to navigate at sea, and birds that fly at night and use the stars to find their way will get lost, too. It'll be a mess! My bag of star dust is around here somewhere. Will you help me find it and stop Jack Frost?"

"Of course we will!" Rachel and Kirsty cried.

Scattered Star Dust

"Thank you, girls," Zara said gratefully.

"We can look for your bag of star dust while we search for the three mystery locations in our orienteering game," Rachel pointed out, turning on her flashlight and shining it onto the map.

"To find the first location, go north, and make sure you don't slip!" Kirsty read. She placed the compass on the map and the three friends watched the needle swing around to point north.

"Make sure you don't slip . . ." Rachel repeated thoughtfully, looking up at the stars. "Oh! I think that means the first place we have to find is right underneath the slipper constellation. That's north from where we're standing."

"Luckily, the slipper still has most of its stars. Let's go right away," Zara suggested.

Quickly Zara flew down to perch on Kirsty's shoulder, hiding behind her hair. Then the girls set off toward the slipper constellation. The other kids, including Alex and Lucas, were still studying their maps, staring at the stars, and trying to figure out how to use the compass. But then Rachel noticed two boys wearing baggy T-shirts, shorts, and baseball caps also heading off in the direction of the slipper constellation. They rudely barged by Alex and Lucas, knocking the map out of Lucas's hand.

"Hey, watch out!" Lucas called. But the two boys didn't stop.

"Looks like those boys figured out where the first location is, too," Rachel remarked as she and Kirsty made their way past the tents.

Suddenly, there was the sound of chirping overhead. Surprised, Rachel and Kirsty glanced up and saw a flock

of little brown birds flying above them.

The birds were tweeting miserably. They kept turning their heads as if they were searching for something.

"Oh, no!" Zara gasped, popping out from behind Kirsty's hair. "This is exactly what I was worried about. These birds are whippoorwills and they fly at night, using the stars to find their way. They're completely lost!"

"Poor things," said Kirsty as the birds flew on, still chirping sadly to one another. "We have to find your bag of magic dust and put the stars back in the right place, Zara."

Zara nodded. "We're almost right underneath the slipper constellation

now," she pointed out.

Rachel was shining her flashlight just ahead of them. "I can see something between the tents!" she said. "It's a sign, and it has a number '1' on it."

"Nice work, girls!" Zara exclaimed. "You found the first location. And just in time, too. . . ."

Rachel and Kirsty looked up at the slipper constellation. They could see several more stars slide away to make up the outline of one of Jack Frost's arms.

"I hope everyone else is able to find it, too," Kirsty said anxiously. "There's hardly any of the slipper left now."

"There's something glowing at the bottom of the sign," Rachel said. "I wonder what it is."

"We saw it first!" yelled a voice behind them.

Zara rushed to hide again as two boys ran out of the shadows and shoved their way past the girls. Rachel recognized them as the same boys who'd pushed Alex and Lucas out of the way earlier.

"Look, prizes!" one of them shouted joyfully. "And they're all for *us*!"

Rachel and Kirsty could see now that there was a pile of glow-in-the-dark star stickers stacked at the bottom of the post for the sign.

"You shouldn't take them all," Rachel called as the two boys grabbed the stickers. "They're supposed to be for everyone."

The boys ignored her and began sticking the stars all over themselves.

Then, shrieking with glee, they ran off.

"That wasn't very nice of them, was it?" Kirsty sighed as the two boys, glowing with stars, disappeared from sight again. "What's the next clue, Rachel?"

Rachel looked at the map. "To find the second location, go west and brush up on your orienteering skills!" she read out.

"West is that way," Kirsty said, staring down at the compass. "And I guess the clue means that we have to look right underneath the stars of the toothbrush constellation!" She peered up at the sky and frowned. "But where is it?"

"It vanished!" Rachel gasped. "Look, Jack Frost has both of his arms now. He must have stolen all the stars from the toothbrush constellation."

"Not quite," Zara chimed in. "I know the usual positions of the stars so well that I can see there's still one part of the toothbrush left. Look at that lone star right there." Zara pointed her wand at a single star twinkling away on its own. "That's what's left of the toothbrush constellation."

Just then the girls heard footsteps behind them, and Zara quickly

fluttered out of sight.

"Hi, you two," Kirsty called as a sad-looking Alex and Lucas came toward them. "How are you doing?"

"Not very well," Lucas sighed. "We were trying to make our way to the first spot under the slipper constellation, but so many of the stars have moved that we're lost."

"You're heading in the right direction," Rachel told them, pointing toward the first sign.

"Thanks!" Lucas and Alex looked more cheerful and rushed off.

"Let's hurry, Rachel," Kirsty said anxiously, "before the last toothbrush star disappears!"

Fixing their eyes on the single star, the girls headed to the west of the campsite.

As they went, they met a bunch of other kids who were lost and confused because of the shifting stars. Each time, Rachel and Kirsty helpfully directed them to the first location.

Then the girls went on their way, using their flashlights to brighten the darkness. Suddenly, Kirsty tripped over something. She gasped, staggered, and almost fell.

"Kirsty, are you OK?" cried Zara, flying off her shoulder.

"I'm fine," Kirsty replied. She pointed her flashlight downward and saw that the laces on one of her sneakers had come undone. Kirsty bent to retie it, but then, to her surprise, she noticed tiny specks of glitter on the ground. "Zara, Rachel, look at this!" she called.

Zara swooped down to see. "That's my star dust!" she exclaimed. "But how did it get there?"

Rachel moved her own flashlight beam slowly across the ground, picking out the specks of fairy dust. "I think they've been stamped into the ground by someone," she declared. "See those big, clumsy footprints?"

"Goblin footprints!" Kirsty gasped. "Those two rude little boys must be goblins in disguise! They're the only ones who are ahead of us."

"And they have my bag of star dust!" Zara added.

Glow-in-the-dark Goblins!

"Well, at least they left a trail of star dust for us to follow to the second location!" Rachel said with a grin. With the flashlight, the three friends could see the path of star dust sparkling into the distance. "Off we go!"

The trail led Zara and the girls through the campsite and toward the entrance to Camp Stargaze.

"I think the second location must be close to the camp gate," Kirsty said. "Look, it's right underneath the only star left of the toothbrush constellation."

"You're right, Kirsty," Rachel added, directing the beam of her flashlight at the camp entrance. "I can see a sign with a '2' on it. There's a big silver foil star tacked on the gate, too."

"And there are the glow-in-the-dark goblins!" Zara whispered.

The goblins, still covered in stickers, were kneeling on the ground under the tall, wooden sign.

They were scooping up handfuls of star-shaped chocolates and shoving them into their pockets.

"More prizes!" yelled the big goblin, who had glowing stars stuck on each ear like giant earrings.

"Stop!" Kirsty called. "That chocolate is for everyone!"

The smaller goblin, who had a star sticker on the end of his long, pointy green nose, scowled at her.

"Go and find your own prizes!" he shouted, grabbing the last few chocolate stars. Then both goblins jumped up and raced off into the dark of the Whispering Woods. Sparkles drifted around them. They were leaving a trail of fairy dust through the trees!

"Girls, I'm going to turn you into fairies," Zara said. "Then we can chase the goblins quickly, and no one will see us." She fluttered above the girls' heads, showering them with fairy magic from her wand. Instantly, Rachel and Kirsty shrank to the same

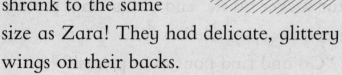

size as Zara! They had delicate, glittery wings on their backs.

"There go the goblins!" Zara called as they saw two glowing figures dart between the trees. "We can follow them easily, even in the dark, because of the star stickers they're wearing. Come on!"

Zara, Rachel, and Kirsty zoomed into

the Whispering Woods. For a minute, they couldn't see the goblins at all, but suddenly Kirsty spotted a faint glow through the undergrowth.

"There they are!" she whispered.

The goblins were running along one of the paths in the woods. Zara and the girls followed them at a safe distance, swerving around the trees and keeping well out of sight. At last, the goblins skidded to a halt beside a tall oak tree. Zara, Rachel, and Kirsty landed on a branch just above their heads and hid among the leaves.

"I think we finally got away from that tricky fairy and her silly friends!" the bigger goblin panted. "Let's eat our chocolate."

Zara and the girls watched as the

goblins sat down under the tree and began to empty their pockets, piling the chocolate stars on the grass. Then they saw the bigger goblin take out a shiny satin bag and throw it on top of the pile of chocolates.

"That's my bag of star dust!" Zara whispered.

The goblins unwrapped some of the chocolate and gobbled it up.

"Jack Frost is going to be very happy to see his constellation," the smaller goblin said smugly. He opened Zara's bag and tossed a handful of magic dust

onto the grass,
where it
sparkled like
tiny jewels.
"Maybe he'll
give us another
prize!"

The bigger goblin didn't answer
because he was cramming another
chocolate star into his already-full
mouth. Just then, Zara and the girls saw
one of the whippoorwills flying toward
them.

Rachel and Kirsty were amazed by
how big the bird was now that they were
the size of fairies. Looking sad, the
whippoorwill landed on the same
branch where the three friends were
perched.

"This poor bird must be lost," Zara whispered.

Suddenly the bird fluttered off the branch again and swooped down to the ground, skimming right over the goblins' heads. The goblins shrieked with fear.

"What's that?" the big goblin wailed through a mouthful of chocolate.

"It must be a pogwurzel!" the other goblin yelled, shivering and shaking all over. "Let's get out of these scary dark woods!"

Quickly, the big goblin grabbed the bag of star dust and the remaining chocolates and they both took off at full speed. Zara, Rachel, and Kirsty flew after them, but then Rachel noticed the beam of a flashlight ahead of them.

"Someone's coming!" she whispered to Zara and Kirsty, and the three of them ducked behind a bush.

A moment later, Peter came down the path and bumped right into the two goblins.

"Aha, so you're the boys who stole

all the prizes!" Peter said angrily as
he spotted the chocolates in the bigger
goblin's arms. Rachel, Kirsty, and Zara
breathed a sigh of relief when they
realized that, although Peter had a
flashlight, the goblins' faces were hidden
in the shadows.

"That's very greedy. Give them back, please." Peter held out his hands.

"My bag of star dust is in the middle of that pile of chocolates!" Zara said anxiously. "We can't let the goblins give it to Peter."

"Don't worry," Rachel replied. "I have an idea. Quick, Zara, make me and Kirsty humans again!"

Scary Shadows

Zara twirled her wand, and Kirsty and Rachel grew back to their normal size in a cloud of fairy dust.

"Hi, Peter," Rachel called, running out from behind the bush. Kirsty followed, wondering what Rachel's plan was. "We found those chocolates in the woods," Rachel went on, "and these boys are helping us carry them back to the signpost by the gate."

"Yes, that's exactly what we're doing!" the small goblin chimed in quickly.

"Oh, so you weren't the ones who took them," Peter said to the goblins. "Sorry about that. OK, make sure you put them back, so the others can find them." With a smile, he walked away. Kirsty and Rachel breathed sighs of relief.

"We just helped you, so now you can help us," Rachel told the goblins. "Give us the bag of star dust, please." She pointed up at the sky where the Jack Frost constellation now had legs.

"The stars need to go back where they belong."

"And you can put the chocolates back, too," Kirsty added.

The goblins glanced at each other. "You have to be kidding!" the smaller goblin yelled. He grabbed some of the chocolates from the other goblin and began throwing them at the girls. The bigger goblin joined in, pelting Rachel and Kirsty so hard that they were forced to run to the bush for cover.

"Stop it!" Zara shouted, flying out

from behind the bush to see what was
going on.

Having used up all the chocolates,
the goblins turned and ran off. The big
goblin was still clutching the bag of star
dust.

"After them, girls!" called Zara,
waving her wand around Rachel and
Kirsty.

When the girls were fairies again, they
all zoomed after the two goblins. They
were running along one of the paths
that led back to Camp Stargaze.

"We won't be able to chase the goblins
through the camp," Rachel pointed out,
dismayed. "Someone might see."

"Maybe we should try to keep
them here in the Whispering Woods,"
Kirsty suggested. "They're nervous

because it's dark and scary."

"You're right, Kirsty," Zara agreed.
"It might be our best chance of getting
my bag away from them. Let's chase the
goblins back into the trees!"

The three friends linked hands and
flew very fast so that they could get in
front of the goblins. Then they swooped
down, hovering in front of them and
blocking their path.

"It's those fairies again!" the bigger
goblin shouted, spinning around.
"Quick, run the other way!" And the

two goblins charged back into the thickest part of the woods.

"Quickly, girls!" Zara whispered.

Rachel, Kirsty, and Zara zoomed around the goblins, herding them deeper into the woods. Whenever one of the goblins tried to take a path that led back to the campsite, Zara and the girls would dart down to block their way.

"But how are we going to get the bag of star dust back?" Kirsty panted as she flew around the goblins' heads. "We need a plan!"

All of a sudden, Kirsty's heart began to pound with fright. A great black shadow was flying through the darkness, heading

straight toward her. Quickly, she
swerved out of its way. When it came
closer, she was very
relieved to see that
it was only one of
the whippoorwills
fluttering through the
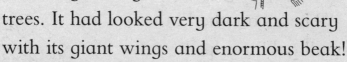
trees. It had looked very dark and scary
with its giant wings and enormous beak!

"Oh!" Kirsty exclaimed, flying over to
Rachel and Zara. "I think I know how
we can get the bag of star dust back
from the goblins!" She took her fairy-
sized flashlight out of her pocket.
"Look . . ."

Kirsty switched on her flashlight and
pointed the beam at Zara. Instantly, a
gigantic shadow with enormous wings
and long arms and legs appeared on the

broad trunk of a tree behind her.

"Look!" the big goblin shouted, pointing at the shadow looming over them. "What's that?"

Rachel grinned. She flew into the light, too, and a second enormous shadow sprang up next to Zara's.

"There's another!" the small goblin yelped.

With a quick flick of her wand, Zara spun a cloud of magical fairy dust around herself and the girls.

"WE'RE WATCHING

YOU!" Zara called to the goblins. But her spell had changed her sweet, silvery voice to a loud, scary roar.

"YOU SHOULDN'T HAVE STOLEN ALL THE PRIZES!" said Rachel, trying not to laugh as her voice, now as loud and frightening as Zara's, boomed through the air. "THAT WAS NOT VERY NICE!"

"They must be pogwurzels!" the big goblin wailed, terrified. "And they're not just pogwurzels," moaned the small

goblin. "They're *giant* pogwurzels!
Help!"

Rachel turned on her flashlight, too.
Then she, Kirsty, and Zara took turns
flying around in front of the beams of
light, casting their huge shadows all
over the trees around them. The goblins
moaned with fear and clung to each
other, their knees knocking together.

"DROP THE BAG OF STAR DUST, AND WE'LL LET YOU GO!" Kirsty roared in her pogwurzel voice.

The girls both held their breaths. Would the goblins give in and return Zara's bag?

Starry
Party

The goblins stared at each other in a
panic.

"What should we do?" groaned the
big goblin. "Jack Frost will be really
angry if his constellation disappears!"

"Do you want to get eaten by
pogwurzels instead?" the small goblin
demanded. "Which is worse—Jack Frost
or pogwurzels?"

The big goblin hesitated for a moment. Then he yelled, "Pogwurzels!" Quickly he threw the bag high in the air toward the giant shadows, and he and his friend ran off through the trees.

Smiling, Zara zoomed over and tapped the bag with her wand. It immediately shrank down to fairy-size and Zara caught it in her hand. "We did it, girls!" Zara declared happily. "Now everything in the night sky will soon be back to normal. Let's go and see."

Rachel and Kirsty followed Zara as she flew upward through the trees.

Then they hovered above the Whispering Woods, staring at the sky. The stars were already sliding away from Jack Frost's arms and legs and back to their own constellations. As the girls watched, Jack Frost gradually got smaller and smaller until only his icy grin was left. Soon, even that was gone.

"All the stars are back in the right place." Rachel sighed happily. "The night sky looks beautiful."

"And the birds can find their way again," Kirsty added as the flock of whippoorwills swooped past them, calling happily to each other.

"I want to give everyone in Fairyland the good news," Zara said as they floated down and landed at the edge of the woods. She showered her magic fairy dust over the girls and they instantly became humans again. "Thank you, girls. You're both stars! Keep up the good work!"

Rachel and Kirsty waved good-bye as Zara vanished in a mist of golden sparkles.

"Look, the pajamas constellation is the only one on the map left to find now,

and it's right above the observatory," Rachel pointed out as they went back to camp.

"And there's the third sign outside the observatory door," said Kirsty. "This is the last location."

All the other kids, including Alex and Lucas, were also heading to the observatory.

"Now that the stars are back in their place, everyone can follow their maps!" Kirsty whispered to Rachel as Peter gathered everyone together.

"Nice work!" Peter said. "Can anyone put the three locations together and solve the puzzle?"

Everyone started talking, trying to work it out.

"The first location was in the camp by

the tents," Kirsty murmured to Rachel.

"The second was the gate with the silver star on it," said Rachel.

"And the third was the observatory," Kirsty added. "And we gaze at the stars from the observatory, so it must be—"

"CAMP STARGAZE!" the girls called together.

"You got it!" Peter said, and everyone applauded. "Now, come into the observatory. Professor Hetty and I have a surprise for you."

Everyone crowded into the observatory where Professor Hetty was waiting for them. The walls were decorated with glow-in-the-dark stars and there was a

table set up with sandwiches and cakes.

"It's a starry party!" Professor
Hetty laughed, handing out glasses
of punch. "It's been fun watching the
strange events in the sky, but I'm glad
everything's back to normal."

As the party got underway, Rachel
and Kirsty sneaked a peek through the
giant telescope.

"There's Zara!" Kirsty whispered,
pointing to a silver light floating in the
sky.

As the girls watched, the silver light
burst into a shower of sparkles. Then the
sparkles formed
themselves into
a dazzling
constellation
in the shape
of a fairy.
It hung there
glittering in
the sky for a
moment, and then
disappeared.

Rachel and Kirsty glanced at each
other in delight. It was a wonderful
ending to another fairy adventure!

THE NIGHT FAIRIES

Rachel and Kirsty have helped
Zara find her magic dust.
Now it's time to help . . .

Morgan

the Midnight Fairy!

Join their next nighttime adventure
in this magical sneak peek. . . .

The Midnight Hour

"I'm not tired at all, are you?" Kirsty Tate asked her best friend, Rachel Walker. It was late at night and the two girls were in the Whispering Woods, shining their flashlights into the shadows as they collected firewood. They were staying with their families at a vacation spot called Camp Stargaze. Tonight,

the whole camp was having a midnight
feast.

"Not one bit," Rachel replied as
she tugged at a branch from the
undergrowth. "I'm too excited to even
think about being tired!" She grinned
at Kirsty. "What a great vacation this
is turning out to be. A whole week
together, lots of adventures, a midnight
feast, and . . ." She lowered her voice,
cautiously glancing around. "And plenty
of fairy magic, too!"

Kirsty smiled. It was true—she and
Rachel had been having a wonderful
time this week.

It was a chilly night, and Kirsty and
Rachel were happy to see that the moon
and stars were shining brightly. "Zara's
starlight magic is working perfectly

again," Kirsty said, gazing up at the twinkling stars. She gathered some more sticks, humming cheerfully to herself.

Tonight was going to be so much fun! Peter, one of the camp counselors, was lighting a big fire, and then there were going to be lots of fireworks at the stroke of midnight, followed by a feast for everyone.

As the girls made their way through the dark woods, they heard a voice calling: "Kirsty, Rachel, is that you? We found lots of firewood down here!"

"Follow the beams of our flashlights!" shouted a second voice. Then the girls saw bright white beams of light flashing through the trees in the distance. . . .

RAINBOW magic™

There's Magic in Every Series!

The Rainbow Fairies
The Weather Fairies
The Jewel Fairies
The Pet Fairies
The Fun Day Fairies
The Petal Fairies
The Dance Fairies
The Music Fairies
The Sports Fairies
The Party Fairies
The Ocean Fairies
The Night Fairies

Read them all!

SCHOLASTIC

www.scholastic.com
www.rainbowmagiconline.com

RMFAIRY4

RAINBOW magic™

SPECIAL EDITION

Three Books in Each One— More Rainbow Magic Fun!

RAINBOW magic

These activities are magical!
Play dress-up, send friendship notes, and much more!

SCHOLASTIC
www.scholastic.com
www.rainbowmagiconline.com

HIT entertainment

RMACTIV3